TOTO

THE NINJA CAT
AND THE
SUPERSTAR **CAT**ASTROPHE

  This book belongs to:

BY DERMOT O'LEARY

TOTO THE NINJA CAT
AND THE GREAT SNAKE ESCAPE

TOTO THE NINJA CAT
AND THE INCREDIBLE CHEESE HEIST

TOTO THE NINJA CAT
AND THE SUPERSTAR CATASTROPHE

TOTO

THE NINJA CAT
AND THE
SUPERSTAR CATASTROPHE

DERMOT O'LEARY

ILLUSTRATED BY NICK EAST

h HODDER

HODDER CHILDREN'S BOOKS

First published in Great Britain in 2020 by Hodder and Stoughton

1 3 5 7 9 10 8 6 4 2

Text copyright © Dermot O'Leary, 2019
Illustrations copyright © Nick East, 2019
Inside back cover photograph by Ray Burmiston

ISBN 978 1 444 95206 3

Printed and bound in Great Britain by Clays Ltd, Elcograf S.p.A.
The paper and board used in this book are made from wood from
responsible sources

MIX
Paper from
responsible sources
FSC® C104740

Hodder Children's Books
An imprint of Hachette Children's Group
Part of Hodder and Stoughton
Carmelite House
50 Victoria Embankment
London EC4Y 0DZ
An Hachette UK Company
www.hachette.co.uk
www.hachettechildrens.co.uk

TO ANYONE READING
WHO ADOPTS
OR RESCUES ANIMALS –
HUZZAH FOR YOU!

CHAPTER I

Toto knew she had one chance, just one shot at catching the canine ringleaders of an illegal dog-bone syndicate. They'd been stealing London's pooches' **FAVOURITE TREATS** for the last six months, and this was their **BIGGEST SHIPMENT YET.** If she didn't bust them tonight, who knew when she'd get another chance.

The dog-bone-stealing had, of course,

been met with outrage. Unlike cats, who just 'cat up' and get on with it, dogs are far more vocal when they are unhappy. So, London's dog population had been howling at all hours of the night and digging holes everywhere with nothing to put in them. No one in the capital, animals and humans

alike, had been able to get a wink of sleep from the noise and everyone was getting cranky. The pressure was on Toto to solve the crime, and *FAST!*

'Dogs are supposed to be man's best friend and loyal to a fault, but here they are, stealing each other's bones and all for what? Payment in *BISCUITS,* I imagine,' she muttered to herself. She was waiting impatiently for her brother Silver to get back to their hiding place – a rooftop overlooking the warehouse that he was currently in the process of scoping out. They believed this was where the bones were being stored, before being shipped out of London by the gang.

This was her seventh mission since Larry, her boss and head of the UK branch of the **ANCIENT ORDER OF INTERNATIONAL NINJA CATS,** had taken her on as his deputy. She loved being an official **NINJA CAT,** with a little assistance from her trusty brother Silver, who acted as her guide cat, as Toto was almost totally blind. Together they had:

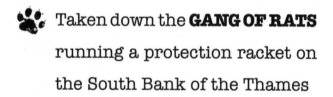

🐾 Taken down the **GANG OF RATS** running a protection racket on the South Bank of the Thames

🐾 Tracked down the **GUINEA PIGS** who were responsible for a massive fraudulent shipment of cucumbers (apparently, they love them – who knew?)

Shut down an illegal **ANT CIRCUS**, which was VERY hard to see, even for Silver

Uncovered corruption at the heart of a beauty pageant for **PUGS**

Solved a mystery involving a **GANG OF EELS** who were master safe-crackers ... slippery!

And now they were on the cusp of smashing an illegal dog-bone-dealing ring.

Larry trusted them – they were succeeding at all the cases he threw their way, and the animals of the UK had never been safer. Life for the kittens was pretty good. The only downside, as far as Toto could tell, was that their names had been in the animal newspaper

The Mammalian Examiner

more than she would have liked. Ninjas really ought to remain incognito! (Although Silver was loving his fan mail ...)

'Piece of cake,' said Silver with a smile, as he jumped back up on to the roof overlooking the warehouse. 'All the bones are in boxes on the ground floor, very

whiffy ... ***DOGS HAVE NO SENSE OF TASTE!***
There are about five dogs, all bull mastiffs
apart from a Jack Russell who, surprise,
surprise, appears to be in charge. This will
be easy enough for you – shimmy over the
wire between here and there, drop in via
the skylight, then just ... do what you do. I'll
signal Sheila and the gang at the front, and
hey presto, we'll be at Catface's for dinner
by eight!'

Sheila was their friend, a police dog who was now head of the **CIA** (Criminal Investigation Animals). They met her when she had helped them foil the **INCREDIBLE CHEESE HEIST.** Together they'd sent the villainous **ARCHDUKE FERDICAT** into hiding. He was last seen floating off into the North Sea on a barge of Camembert cheese. Where he was now was anyone's guess.

Toto worried that one day they'd meet their nemesis again, but for now he seemed to be keeping a very low profile. Since then, they'd worked with Sheila night and day to keep London's animals safe.

Toto laughed and shook her head. 'Oh no, brother, if I'm going over that wire, **YOU ARE COMING WITH ME**; you're not getting out of it that easily! Besides, I might need your eyes once we're inside.'

'Fine,' replied Silver nervously, 'but those dogs look very big and ... toothy.'

Toto patted her brother on the back. 'You take the Jack Russell, I'll deal with the big boys. Come on, let's go.'

Stealthily as ... well, as **NINJAS,** the two cats shimmied across the wire that connected the two rooftops. Toto got across first and dropped down silently, with Silver following just behind.

'Hey, sis, want to see what moves I've been practising?' he whispered.

'What? NO,' mouthed Toto. 'There's a time and a place to show off new skills and this isn't it.'

   But it was too late. Toto's cocky brother
had launched himself through the night sky
and was halfway through a **SOMERSAULT**
(which, to be fair, wasn't half bad) when he
came unstuck. Instead of landing deftly next
to his sister, Silver misjudged the distance

and disappeared

straight

through

the skylight

down on to

the floor

below.

//

Now, the fall itself wasn't too much of a problem; cats are experts at **JUMPING, LANDING** and, in Silver's case, **FALLING.** What was more of a problem were the menacing dogs who quickly got over their surprise and surrounded the intruder. Before they had a chance to speak, however, Silver dusted himself down and took control of the situation … kind of.

'Ladies and gentlemen, a pleasure to make your acquaintance. **SILVERTHORNE'S THE NAME,** I'm here from … I'm here from … err … the Illegal Dog-bone, err, Association, here to make sure that you're trading, err, illegally and above, I mean below board. Do you have the relevant paperwork? It's just a routine check, but **RULES IS RULES.'**

The bull mastiffs all looked at each other, confused and uncertain.

'*WELL, COME ON, I DON'T HAVE ALL NIGHT.*' Silver crossed his arms and tapped his foot impatiently.

Way up above, Toto was listening in horror. *HE'S GOING TO GET HIMSELF TORN LIMB FROM LIMB,* she thought.

But, incredibly, the ruse seemed to be working. Toto had to admit it: he might not be a ninja, but her big brother had the gift of the gab.

'I'm sorry, sir, we'll dig it out now. Here, Derek, where's that manifest of them there bones?' one massive dog called to another.

'I'll just go and have a root around.'

'Best be sharp about it, I wouldn't want to have to fine you,' replied Silver, getting into his part.

'So sorry, sir, we'll have it righ—'

'*WHAT ARE YOU LOT DOING?*' yelled a small and VERY angry Jack Russell as she appeared from an office at the back of the warehouse.

'Oh, guv, this gent is from the ... what was

it?' the bull mastiff asked Silver, nervously.

'The **ILLEGAL DOG-BONE ASSOCIATION,** here to make sure everything is, you know, nice and illegal,' said Silver, who was now looking pretty shifty.

'**YOU IDIOTS!**' yelled the Jack Russell. 'There's no such thing! Or if there is we're not registered with it! I don't know who this joker is, but my money is on the **CIA,** so please do your jobs properly and tear him to shreds.'

Silver gulped as the **MASSIVE SLOBBERING DOGS** formed a circle around him.

'Sorry about this, *sir*, but you know **RULES IS RULES,**' one snarled.

'And *that* is my cue,' Toto said to herself before **DIVING HEADFIRST** through the skylight. The big warehouse was well lit, so she could make out the shadowy shapes below her. As she approached the floor, she righted herself and landed effortlessly on her feet next to her brother, startling the huge dogs.

'Hey, bro, think you can take old

ANGRY-PANTS over there?' She gestured to the Jack Russell. 'And I'll handle these bully boys?'

'You bet, sis ... well, I mean I'll try,' replied Silver.

'Alrighty then ... **LET'S GET NINJA-ING!**'

And with that she set about the dogs. With a **ROUNDHOUSE KICK** here, a **SWEEP OF THE LEGS** there and select use of the **VENTURA SHUFFLE** (Toto's personal favourite, picked up from and named after her old sensei in Italy, involving exactly twenty-four delicate kicks followed by pushing your opponent over with a single claw). In no time, all were lying groggily around her.

Silver, on the other hand, was finding it slightly tougher going against the wiry Jack Russell, who could certainly look after herself. The cat was trying his hardest, but the Jack Russell had him on his back.

'I DON'T SUPPOSE WE PASSED THE INSPECTION,' the Jack Russell laughed, her jaws snapping at Silver's neck.

'No, your customer service leaves a great deal to be desired,' said Toto with a **FLYING KICK** that sent the Jack Russell tumbling into a pile of bones.

Toto helped her brother to his feet as the front doors were smashed open by Sheila and her fellow dog officers from the CIA. **'SHEILA SNARLINGFOOT, CIA. THIS IS A RAID ...'**

She tailed off as she looked at the scene of devastation around her.

'Well done, cats,' she said, obviously impressed.

'Yep, we got them good,' replied an exhausted Silver, getting to his feet. 'Sheila, you can take it from here, right?'

Toto shook at her head and laughed at her brother's bare-faced cheek.

The cats stumbled out of the warehouse, with Toto supporting her brother, who was clutching his bruised ribs. The rest of the CIA team entered and set about arresting the dogs (and gleefully helping themselves to a bone or two). Larry, Toto's boss, was leaning up against a nearby wall watching the whole scene with great admiration.

'*YOU'VE DONE IT AGAIN, CATS ...* what's that? Seven major crimes foiled in as many months? Toto – and yes, you, Silver – have my gratitude. I don't remember a time when the animal population was as safe as it has been since you came on the scene.'

'Thanks, boss,' replied Silver. 'That one

was a toughie, but we nailed it – right, sis?'

Toto laughed. 'Sure thing, Silver.'

Larry patted her shoulder knowingly. He knew that she did all the hard work, but he also knew that Silver was an **INVALUABLE** member of the team.

'Well, I think **BOTH** of you deserve a bit of a **HOLIDAY** now, so take a couple of weeks off and put your paws up, OK?'

The cats nodded vigorously. Toto had to admit, she was a ninja, but she was also a cat ... and really anything under twenty hours sleep a night was an **AFFRONT TO THEIR CAT RIGHTS.** After months of hard work, she was more than ready for a break.

'Now, as for tonight, I've come to escort you to dinner. You might remember we all had a date with a certain Mr Catface?'

'YES!'
shouted Silver.

'LETS EAAAAAAAAAAATTTTTTTTTT!'

The dinner was at the royal palace of Ratborough where Catface's father, king of one of the five rat districts of London, resided.

Ratborough was a subterranean town and the capital of Rat London. It was (by rat standards) beautiful and ornate. The centrepiece was the **ROYAL PALACE,** an enormous building made entirely of see-through glass cola bottles (stunning to look at, but it made going to the loo a little bit embarrassing).

The kittens had met **CATFACE** as soon as they arrived in London from Italy, and he'd been their best friend ever since. He was a rat who also identified as a cat, and he seemed to know, and be liked by, every animal in London. He was **INCREDIBLY STYLISH,** getting all his clothes from a family of foxes who ran a tailor's on Savile Row, **VERY FRIENDLY** and, although he was rubbish at fighting, he had the **HEART OF A LION.** He'd been particularly helpful in tracking down Archduke Ferdicat when this dangerous ex-ninja tried to steal all the cheese in the world.

Catface also put on a **GREAT SUPPER CLUB!** His diet was more cat than rat, and so the cats were tucking into the finest chicken soup, a glorious joint of roast beef with all the trimmings (plus a bowl of cheesy pasta, just for Toto … her favourite), and for dessert a **MASSIVE CHEESECAKE,** all washed down with so much milk you'd

have thought Catface owned his own cow.
(He didn't, but he had a very good friend in
a small farm just north of London – a Dutch
Friesian called Mila, who did him a good
deal on her milk.)

Silver quickly finished off his portion
and then made a start on a platter of the
disgusting scrap burgers that rats absolutely
love, but no self-respecting cat would touch.
No one was entirely sure about what went
into them, but Silver didn't care; he was
stuffing his face and loving it.

Also at the feast were:

🐾 Catface's dad, his rat highness
**HENRICH RATTINOFF THE
835TH** (who was a bit of a

coward and a pompous old
windbag, but not a bad sort)

 **LARRY**

A very hungry **SHEILA**, who'd
arrived late after filing her
paperwork from the crime scene

After the meal had concluded and everyone
had had their fill (apart from Silver, who was
on his twelfth scrap burger), glasses were
chinked and Catface stood up to address his
guests.

'My *DEAR FRIENDS,* I trust you've all
dined well, and enjoyed the delights of the
finest table in Ratborough ...'

'**HUZZAH!**' the king exclaimed loudly, wobbling slightly on his chair. He sounded to Toto like he'd had one too many milks and was due a lie-down.

'Thank you, Father.' Catface raised his glass with a nod before continuing, 'As you all know, ***THE STREETS OF ANIMAL LONDON HAVE NEVER BEEN SO SAFE,*** and whilst we can all take a little credit for this ...'

'Well, I don't like to boast,' the king blustered.

Catface rolled his eyes. 'We can especially thank two Italian cats who have recently come into our lives, captured our hearts, and are the best deputies Larry could have dared to wish for.'

'*HEAR, HEAR!*' The room erupted.

'And ... since your boss has declared you are getting a much-needed holiday ...'

I know, I can't wait, thought Toto. **SLEEP, CLEAN, EAT, REPEAT!**

'... I took it upon myself to get you a little treat. I know you haven't seen much of the countryside in your adopted home and it just so happens that there is a rather special event happening this weekend for which

I have procured three tickets. Cats, we ... are ... going ... to ... **CATSTONBURY!**' At that, Catface sat down and looked very pleased with himself.

'AWESOME!' said Silver. 'What is it?'

'IT?!' replied Catface, standing up again, aghast. 'It's the premier and longest-running **ANIMAL MUSIC FESTIVAL** in the world.

Tens of thousands of animals of all shapes and sizes come from all over the globe, to play music and see the sights. Tickets are like **GOLD DUST,** but I happen to know the organisers – a lovely family of otters. The daughter, Lutra, is a good friend of mine – our fathers used to fish together. She's sorted us out tickets and a **NICE BIG TIPI** to sleep in ... Plus, headlining on the main stage are the hottest band in the world right now: **JONNY AND THE SHORTHAIRS!**'

'NEVER HEARD OF THEM, AND I DON'T KNOW WHAT AN OTTER IS, BUT WE'RE IN!' yelled Silver as he high fived Catface. 'Right, sis?'

Toto hesitated. After all her hard work, she was shattered and the last thing she wanted to do was traipse around a field. But Catface had gone to all this trouble, and her brother was so excited, and she did love it when her human mamma and papa played music at home ... She took a breath then said with a smile, **'WE'RE IN.'**

'Excellent, we'll meet at Paddington station, animal entrance at 5 p.m. tomorrow. Dress code: **FESTIVAL CHIC!'**

CHAPTER 2

'Toto! Silver! I say, over here!' cried Catface, waving at his young friends.

The cats had reached Paddington station, the great Victorian gateway to the west of Britain. They were old hands at using the **ANIMAL TUBE** now, which was how most animals travelled around the big city of London. But the main Paddington terminal was a whole new experience. They had exited the Animal Tube right below platform number one where a **GIGANTIC, HISSING LOCOMOTIVE** stood waiting. It looked very fancy, with shining wooden doors and window frames, and carriages painted in a regal racing green.

'It's much bigger than the Tube, sis,' said Silver, in awe.

Both cats were very excited to be taking their first real train journey, especially as it was taking place overnight in a sleeper carriage. Catface had explained that this was a particularly wonderful train – a vintage Belmond Pullman, which humans only used for **SPECIAL OCCASIONS**.

They trotted over to their friend. Toto had to admit, her early fears had been replaced with excitement about her first music festival. As always, Catface was dressed like the **ECCENTRIC** English gentleman he was. He wore a pale-yellow linen suit, his trademark cravat, trousers that were

PSSSSST

tucked into knee-high cream socks, a pair of brown brogues and a waxed green peak cap. He looked both **COOL** and **ODD,** which kind of summed him up!

'My friends, where are your festival outfits?' he asked with a tinge of disappointment in his voice.

'Well,' Toto began, 'we didn't really know what you meant by **"FESTIVAL CHIC".** And, more importantly, we don't own any clothes ...'

'Hmm, that is an excellent point. I suppose fur does the trick, eh? Still, no matter, we'll get you some suitable attire on site. **LET'S GET ON BOARD,** shall we?'

Silver gulped and began to climb on to the roof of the carriage, which is where they sat when they used the Animal Tube.

'Silver, where the devil are you going?' asked Catface.

'Err, I'm boarding the train ... aren't I?'

'Oh no,' Catface laughed, 'we don't travel on the roof! We'd get blown right off in the outside world.'

Catface climbed on to the wheelset of the train and opened a small door, just below the human doors, about cat height in size. He leant back, took his hat off and waved it in the air.

'No, my friends: today, we travel in **STYLE!** Follow me,' he said grandly, then disappeared through the tiny entrance.

The cats eagerly climbed up on to the wheelset and poked their heads through the small door. 'Oh, sis, you are going to **LOOOOVE** this!' Silver smiled.

Silver described what he could see to his sister. There was a narrow corridor lined with dark mahogany walls and dimmed yellow wall lights. Several doors were open along the carriage, all of which opened to small but cosy-looking berths, each with two single beds **AND AN ORNATE SINK.**

The cats padded excitedly down the corridor and found their cabin. (And, being kittens, they immediately had a quick jump on their beds.)

The train was abuzz with activity. Conductors were **CHECKING TICKETS,** guards were making sure all the animals

found their seats and cabins, porters were **CARRYING LUGGAGE** and haughty waiters carrying silver trays of **DELICIOUS FOOD** were scurrying to and fro.

As the train began to pull out of the station, the conductor took to the tannoy.

'Welcome aboard the

GRAND WEST COUNTRY EXPRESS.

First-class passengers at the rear, restaurant and **AWARD-WINNING MILK BAR** towards the centre of the train. Please keep any territorial spraying to a minimum, and litter trays can be found at the end of every carriage. First stop: Reading. This train terminates at **OTTERVIL,** for the wonderful music festival of **CATSTONBURY.** Allllll paws aboard.'

Excitedly, the cats set off to find Catface. They came to the packed restaurant car, which was filled with booths and a curved milk bar in the corner. A tuxedoed dachshund was currently mixing Catface a creamtail (the animal version of a cocktail) in a martini glass.

'Kittens, you have to try this! **TIMOTHY** makes the most fabulous **CREAMTAIL.** Half Jersey milk, half Brittany cream, with just a soupçon of crème fraiche ... superb. Timothy, line 'em up.'

The cats licked their lips expectantly.

'Very good, sir,' the impassive hound replied.

'So, what do you make of our humble abode for the night? Not the worst digs in the world, what?' The contented cat-rat smiled.

'Catface, **THIS IS THE BEST**, thank you so much,' Toto replied as her drink was passed to her.

'Pish, it's noth—' Catface gasped suddenly as he glanced over the cats' shoulders. 'Oh, my word, it's **JONNY AND THE SHORTHAIRS!**'

'Oh, yeah, wow,' said Silver. 'Err, so, who are they again?'

'Who are they? **WHO ARE THEY?** They are the greatest animal rock band on the planet. It used to be **ERIC AND THE ARTHROPODS**, but their stuff has gone really experimental now, and Eric's ballooned ... owns too many webs, you see, always stuffing his face with flies.'

The cats looked at each other, confused, but they were used to feeling this way around Catface.

'Hmm,' he continued, 'Jonny and the Shorthairs are definitely the best now. They burst on to the scene a year ago and have already had five number one hits. Apparently, they're premiering their brand-new song, **"YOU GOT THE CREAM"**, at Catstonbury. It's going to be epic. I hear the video is hypnotising.'

The cats turned to see what all the fuss was about. Flanked by several massive feline security guards and a suave-looking manager, five shorthaired cats were sat in a booth further down the carriage. At the centre of the booth sat the tallest and most handsome of the cats, almost blonde in colour, with a huge cat quiff, a black bomber jacket and at least six long necklaces – it had to be *JONNY* himself.

'We *have* to go and say hello,' said Catface excitedly, losing all sense of cool. 'Come on, kittens, I bet he'd love to hear about all your ninja stuff.'

'Wait, no ... Catface, that's not ... *WE'RE SUPPOSED TO BE SECRET!*' But Toto was too late – her friend was already dragging the cats along to the band's booth.

'Err, excuse me, Mr, err, Shorthair? I was wondering if it would be OK to say hello?'

'Push off,' said an enormous, gruff cat security guard. 'Mr Shorthair is busy, and does not have time for—'

'Nah, man, let them through,' came a drawl from the middle of the booth.

The cordon of muscle cats parted and the cats were let through, and sat down with the band. There was something about the smell around the booth that Toto found

UNNERVINGLY FAMILIAR, but she couldn't quite place it.

'I've gotta keep the fans happy, right? I guess you must be pretty excited to meet me, yeah? I could hardly make it on to the train through the mob of animals wanting my pawprint,' Jonny said as he absently strummed a guitar. 'Let me introduce my band: on drums, **GINGER**; on keys, **CHRISSIE**; on bass, **NANAR**; and on guitar, **PRISCILLA.** Oh, ha ha, forgot the most important one ... **ME!**'

His band all laughed, but Toto thought it sounded a bit forced.

'This guy loves himself,' she whispered to her brother. But Silver, elbows on the table, cupping his head in his paws, seemed in a daze, already as entranced by the rocker as Catface.

'So, you're off to the festival, yeah? Bet you can't wait to see me – I mean *us* – headline tomorrow night. Yeah, I love Catstonbury, no other music festival like it ... And this year is going to be epic, this new song and video we're dropping is out of this world, life-changing, yeah, it's going to **CHANGE THE PLANET FOR EVER.**'

The rest of the band looked a little doubtful, but Jonny was oblivious to them.

'So, tell me about you guys ... and why you think I'm so great, ha ha,' he crooned.

'Cripes!' said Catface as he introduced himself. 'I've been a fan since the start, know all of the words to all of the hits ...

"*SCRATCH MY SOFA UP*" has always been my favourite. But my friends here, Toto and Silver, are new to the whole festival scene, and your set will be their first time listening to your music. I just know they're going to love it.'

'Wait, *TOTO AS IN TOTO THE NINJA CAT?*' said Jonny's bass player, Nana, a black cat wearing a stylish leather jacket. 'Jonny, this is the one I've seen on the news fighting crime, and that's her brother.'

'That's right,' said Silver, beaming. 'I'm pretty much a fully fledged ninj—'

'Actually, I don't mean to be rude, but it's supposed to be a *SECRET ORDER,* so we're really not supposed to talk about it,' interrupted Toto.

'Hey, little guy, chill,' Jonny said with his hands up.

'*Girl!*' Toto corrected.

'Yeah, girl, whatever ... Don't get your long hair in a twist, we're cool here, and you know you're amongst stars, so we're all famous. Well, some of us more than others, right, guys?!'

His bandmates laughed again, but Toto decided it was **DEFINITELY** forced this time – like they knew they had to join in. Jonny high fived all his security guards.

This guy is insufferable, thought Toto.

'Now, Nana here says you're some kind of ninja, that's cool, I can dig that, I do a bit of **KICK-BOXING** myself.' At this, he sprang from his booth out into the aisle, where the whole carriage could see him.

'Check this out,' he said boastfully, and proceeded to execute a couple of *just* about passable high kicks and punches into thin air. **'*HIYAH! OHHH YEAH!*'** he shouted, really getting into it.

The whole carriage was in raptures, clapping and whooping. Jonny lapped up the attention.

'OK, fella, let's see some of your skills – let's spar,' he said to Toto.

Toto was getting a little frustrated at the feline show-off.

'Well, firstly, like I *did* say thirty seconds ago, I am a *girl*, and secondly, you might have heard if you were listening to anyone else than yourself, I'm actually part of a

SECRET ancient order. We only use our powers when there's no other option, so it would be against my code to show off.'

'Toto! Surely just a couple of moves? It couldn't hurt ...' cried Catface, with Silver nodding eagerly over his shoulder.

'No, guys, don't force the little one. It's cool, all good. Some people are meant to be stars and others, backing singers. I just wanted to test those ninja reactions. Hey, Toto, watch this!'

Jonny aimed a roundhouse kick in her direction. Even with her poor eyesight she could see, hear and feel the kick coming a mile off, and ducked easily out of the way. Jonny's leg sailed right over her, and he ended up sprawling on the floor.

WOOOSH

Jonny's burly security guards all rushed to help him back on to his feet. The whole carriage was staring, hushed and nervous about what would happen next.

Toto could tell Jonny was livid that his pride had been stung. She could feel his anger towards her. But he recovered his composure quickly. 'Hey, no harm done,' he said through clenched teeth. 'I knew that move would be too easy for the little dude, did it deliberately, just, err, wanted to see how quick those reactions were ... It's cool! Come on gang, let's party!' At this he turned his back on the ninja and returned to his table.

Catface was oblivious to the situation. Silver, though, reached out to his sister pleadingly, but Toto had had enough. 'I'm going to turn in,' she said and quickly made her way back to her cabin, unaware that she was under the **WATCHFUL STARE** of Jonny's security guards.

As she tucked herself into her bed in her snug cabin, she had a **NAGGING,**

UNEASY FEELING. It wasn't just Jonny; her **NINJA SENSE OF DANGER** was working in overdrive. She couldn't quite put her paw on why, but she had a horrible feeling that this trip was going to be far from the fun-filled couple of days Catface had planned.

CHAPTER 3

The sleek train sped past the West London suburbs and into the rolling fields of the English countryside. As the mid-summer sun set, the gentle rocking motion of the carriage lulled Toto into a deep slumber. She fell into a dream that there was a huge plate of **CAMEMBERT** in front of her. The **GOOEY FRENCH CHEESE** had been one of her favourites, but she hadn't been able to stomach it since her duel on board a barge full of the stuff, when she had almost been slain by **ARCHDUKE FERDICAT.** In her dream, the Camembert on her plate grew in size until it covered the table, then the floor. It began to ooze through the cracks in the door and the windows and it kept growing until the **WHOLE ROOM** was filled with the **OVERWHELMING SMELL** and she had to leap on to the chandelier to escape and—

A jolt from the giant locomotive awoke her. She sat bolt upright, the sun now long gone, replaced by a **CLOUDLESS MOONLIT SKY** which illuminated the cabin and made it easier for her to get her bearings.

Rubbing the sleep from her eyes, she glanced over at the other bed in the berth where she could make out the shape of her brother, curled around his own bushy tail, fast asleep and **SNORING GENTLY.** *No waking you – belly full of milk, I'd imagine*, she thought. She lay back on her bed and tried to drift off again ... looking out the window, up at the ceiling, and around the cabin. She could make out the shadowy shapes of the beautiful iron luggage rack above her, the white porcelain washbasin and, in the corner of the room, the tall hat stand that—

Wait a minute! she thought. *There was no hat stand there when I came to bed.*

The ninja **LEAPED OUT OF HER BED**

just in time as the hat stand came to life and brought a lethal wooden rolling pin **CRASHING** down, missing Toto by a hair's breadth and **SMASHING** the bedside lamp.

The hat stand – which, it was now obvious to Toto, was actually a **GIGANTIC SIBERIAN CAT** – looked down and sneered, 'I'm the ticket inspector! And it looks like you don't have a valid one to be on this train.'

He cackled and took another swing at Toto's head. Once more she evaded the blow and dived across to her brother's bed, accidentally landing with one foot on his head.

Although Toto knew she had to think of something fast, she was momentarily distracted:

HOW

IN THE

WORLD

WAS SILVER

STILL ASLEEP?

She'd just landed on his head, was standing now with one paw right in his ear and he was still snoring away like he was back in his basket at home!

'I heard you were fast, but come on, where are you going to run to? My boss says you have to get off this train, so be a good girl and let me crack you over the head with this and chuck you out the window so we can all get on with our evening,' the henchcat grumbled.

The window! Toto thought. That's my chance. In these close quarters Toto knew she could use hardly any of her **NINJA MOVES,** but she had windows and walls to bounce off and sometimes that's all a ninja needs.

Her assailant approached her menacingly, thinking he had her cornered. He raised the rolling pin to deliver a deadly blow.

Just as the wooden bat was about to make contact with Toto, she used her **STILL** sleeping brother as a **SPRINGBOARD,** pushing him to safety with her hind legs and launching herself through the cabin and out of harm's way, as the rolling pin connected harmlessly with the fluffy pillow. The lumbering henchcat had made a **BIG MISTAKE,** using the full weight of his body on the blow. Toto knew he was now off balance. Sensing her chance, she jumped up to the window, deftly unlocking and opening it. Then she pushed off towards the henchcat, and before he knew what had hit him ... she hit him ... right in the jaw! The blow sent him bouncing off a wall, spinning right around so that he faced the open window.

He was dizzy and dazed, so a simple kick up the bottom sent him screaming, tumbling out on to the verge below.

'*SORRY TO DISAPPOINT YOU, BUT IT'S NOT MY STOP YET!*' Toto called out to him as she closed the window, feeling very pleased with herself. She looked around to see Silver on the floor, still snoring his head off. 'I wish someone had been awake to hear that,' she muttered.

'Someone tried to *THROW YOU OFF THE TRAIN?* Toto, that's absurd,' exclaimed a bleary-eyed Catface, as he pulled off his eye mask and whisker net, swung his legs off his bed and grabbed his crimson silk nightgown.

When Toto had **FINALLY** raised Silver from his slumber, he was more confused about waking up on the floor and why Toto had the window open (**'MAMMA MIA,** I'll catch my death of cold. It's not Italy you know!') than anything else. The cats had made their way down the corridor to their friend's cabin, to see if he could help make sense of this all.

'Are you sure you weren't dreaming? You know, you've been so busy and tired lately, maybe your mind is playing tricks on you?' her friend suggested sympathetically.

'No! Well, I *was* dreaming, about Camembert, weirdly, but it wasn't that. Listen, I think maybe Jonny had something to do with this.'

'Oh, Toto, that's too much. Why on earth would Jonny want you hit over the head with a rolling pin and thrown off the train?' Catface was starting to sound a bit peeved.

'Look, I know it sounds crazy, but when I dodged out of the way of his kick he was furious.'

'Silver, did you see any of this attack tonight?'

'Hmm, I was VERY tired, you see, so I sort of slept through all of it. Sorry, sis,' Silver said, shrugging his shoulders.

'There you have it – surely even Silver would have woken up if there was a fight going on over his head? I'm sure you just had a *TERRIBLE NIGHTMARE.'* Catface put an arm around her shoulders, and gave her a comforting squeeze. But then he added in a gentle tone, 'You really can't go around hurling accusations at the biggest superstar in the world, Toto. I hate to ask this, but might you be a tad jealous of Jonny?'

Toto was dismayed. 'Catface, are you mad? I'm a member of a **SECRET ORDER**, I'm not even supposed to be known, let alone **WANT** to be famous. It's not my fault that we've been on the telly and have loads of hits on **CATTUBE.** Everyone films everything nowadays.'

'Well, she's right there. There always seems to be someone filming when we've made a bust. I have to say I, for one, find our growing fame very, err, *stressful*,' Silver said, not quite convincingly.

'All I'm saying,' countered Catface, 'is that your nose might be a liiittle out of joint. I wouldn't blame you, Toto. **JONNY IS THE BIGGEST SUPERSTAR** on the planet right now – it's OK to feel intimidated.'

Toto couldn't believe it – why wasn't her best friend taking her seriously? How could she possibly be jealous of an **IDIOTIC ROCK STAR** who was clearly in love with himself? She was certain that her run-in with Jonny had something to do with her attack, but how could she prove it?

'Now, my friends,' said Catface, 'go back to your cabin, get some sleep and we'll put this whole episode down to a **BAD DREAM** and enjoy our weekend, yes?'

Toto was crestfallen, but couldn't argue any more. Just as the cats were about to leave, there was a knock at the door.

'Enteeerrr,' cried Catface, sounding like a town crier.

The door opened slowly to reveal Jonny's manager, who they'd seen earlier. Dressed in all black, he wore a peacoat, a roll-neck sweater, shades and a flat cap. He leaned up against the door frame in a very cool manner.

'Good evening, sorry to disturb you. My team heard some **COMMOTION** and wanted to check that everything was all right,' he said, as he casually examined his claws. 'Jonny wanted me to check on you personally.'

'No problem at all, just a bad dream, isn't that right, Toto?' said Catface.

'Yeah, something like that,' replied Toto, staring at the floor.

'Oh, we all get those ... I have nightmares about **STORMS AT SEA** myself ...' he said deliberately, as his eyes bored into Toto. 'I'll leave you to get back to bed. Sleep well and watch out for those windows. I hear the locks can be very loose ... wouldn't want anyone **FALLING OUT OF THE TRAIN**, would we?' He let his words hang in the air for a moment, before turning and walking slowly down the corridor, whistling a Jonny and the Shorthairs song to himself.

'**WELL, HE WAS CHARMING**,' said Catface. 'See, Jonny himself wanted to make sure you were all right, sent his manager, no less! Now back to bed you two, we'll be pulling into **CATSTONBURY** in a matter of hours, so go and get some shuteye.'

The two small cats made their way down the carriage back to their cabin.

'Come on, sis, let's try to enjoy this weekend off. Catface is right, we've been working so hard, you probably just had a nightmare.'

Toto said nothing. She knew that it was no dream, and everything Jonny's manager had said seemed **VERY FISHY** to her – plus, there was that familiar smell again! It was no use saying anything more to Catface or her brother – she would need some kind of proof to convince them. But, more importantly, she knew that she needed to keep all her **NINJA SKILLS ON FULL ALERT.** Whoever had wanted to get rid of her had failed, but she knew it wouldn't be the last time they tried.

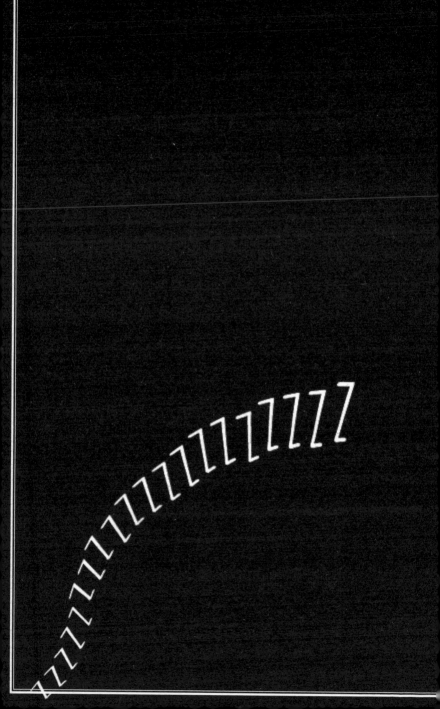

ZZZZZZZZZZZZZZZ

CHAPTER 4

The rest of the night passed uneventfully, and Toto was even able to get a couple of hours' sleep.

The cats woke to Catface knocking gently on their door, bringing them each a mug of warm milk. As the sun rose over the West Country fields, they felt the train start to slow and eventually it hissed to a stop. **THEY HAD REACHED OTTERVIL!**

'Righty-ho, my friends.' Catface slapped his knees. 'We must be hasty with our ablutions, our transport to the festival awaits!'

Minutes later, the small felines and their friend hopped off the train, and it pulled away in a cloud of dust, leaving a platform full of animals of all shapes and sizes to file out of the quaint, red-brick station, where **A FLEET OF SHETLAND PONIES** decked in white and yellow flowers were waiting to transport the festivalgoers to site.

Jonny and the band had already been whisked away by his security and were making their way to the festival in true rock-star style, flown by air in woven baskets carried by serious-looking common buzzards.

'Now, our lift should be along any minute ... Ah, here we are, right on cue!' Catface took off his hat and waved at the strange sight coming into view.

A huge powerful St Bernard dog was towing what looked like a **_BACK-TO-FRONT WHEELBARROW,_** ridden by an otter wearing a blue and white checked neck scarf.

'Lutra!' Catface cried. 'Over here!'

'Catface, my dear friend, so good to see you,' the otter called, as she dismounted the wheelbarrow. 'And, finally, I get to meet the two cats you've been telling me so much about. Toto and Silver, welcome to **CATSTONBURY!** It's such a pleasure to have you with us this weekend.' She hugged the cats warmly.

'*SO THAT IS AN OTTER!*' whispered Toto to her brother. 'I've never smelled a scent quite like it … a little bit of fast-flowing river with a dash of earthy woodiness – lovely.'

Silver leaned in close to add quietly, 'Oh yeah, the hair, the fur, those eyes – she's really pretty. I think Catface might have the hots for her!'

'Let's get going, I don't want you guys to miss a thing.' Lutra helped the cats to clamber into the wheelbarrow and called out, 'Full steam ahead, Gregory!'

'All right, all right, I'll go as fast as I can.' The long-suffering St Bernard winked at the cats.

The guests settled into the cushioned barrow and felt the warm country breeze in their whiskers as they trundled along the lanes that led to the festival and – *hopefully* – a weekend of excitement.

Toto started to relax. She tried to put the incident on the train behind her. With all the crimes she had solved in the last six months there could be scores of baddies looking to get even. Maybe it had nothing to do with Jonny. She told herself to forget about the pampered rock star, and resolved to focus on having a couple of days of *FUN.*

The annual animal music festival of Catstonbury had been held on the same site down in the West Country for nearly fifty years. Started by Lutra's grandad, her parents had picked up the baton and, for the last five years, the young otter herself had taken the reins.

As otters had founded it, the festival had originally been called Otterfest. It was a place where all animals came to enjoy music, poetry, theatre and great food and drink. Everyone was welcome, be they city-dwelling dogs, felines or budgies, country weasels, foxes or voles. But given their love for all music, one animal in particular came to dominate the early days of the festival and so the otters, being a generous bunch, changed the name of the festival to the infamous moniker it enjoys today: **CATSTONBURY!**

The beauty of the festival, for those animals who lived with humans, was that a famous human music festival was held half a mile away at exactly the same time. So, all the pets that came knew their music-loving owners would be none the wiser if they were also away for a couple of days.

Lutra was finishing up explaining the history of the festival to the cats as Gregory reached the crest of a hill. Silver gave a little gasp as the festival site came into view.

'**SIS, THIS PLACE IS SOMETHING ELSE.**' He quickly described all he could see to his sister. The green fields swept down ahead of them, carpeted with tents of all shapes and sizes, some big enough to hold packs of dogs, others that were the size of an ant colony. There were food stalls that catered for every animal's taste, covered in flags and bunting that glittered in the sunlight. Snaking through the festival site was a crystal-clear river that led to a wood in the far distance, and right in the centre of the field on the river bank was a **MASSIVE STAGE,** with two huge cat ears at the very top.

'**THE HOLT STAGE,**' said Lutra. 'It's *the* legendary stage for any animal musician to headline. It's been the heart of the festival right back to the days of 'Paws Robinson' in the 1970s. They say if you play the Holt Stage, you've made it. That's where **JONNY AND THE SHORTHAIRS** will be playing tonight. He loves himself a bit too much, in my opinion,' she said giving Toto a little nudge, 'but you can't deny he gets the crowd going. This place will be rocking tonight. Now let's find your tipi.'

She was about to take the cats to their tent when they heard a thud from underneath the wheelbarrow.

'**OUCH!**' A small white and tabby cat crawled out, rubbing his bottom.

Lutra shook her head. 'Socks, you cheeky little stowaway! Were you holding on to the underside of the wheelbarrow the whole way? I told you last year: buy a ticket, or at least ask me and I'll get you one! I should have you thrown out ...' But the hopeful, pleading expression on Socks' face seemed to be quickly melting her resolve, and she said, **'OH, COME HERE AND GIVE ME A CUDDLE.'**

'Cheers, Lutra,' he said in a strong London accent, as he nuzzled the otter. 'More fun sneaking in.'

It was clear to the cats that this tiny kitten was cheeky, confident and a bit of a handful ... they liked him immediately.

''Ello, Catface, me old china. And this must be Toto and Silver – delighted, I'm sure,' he said with a bow.

'**YOUNG MASTER SOCKS.**' Catface smiled indulgently. 'Cats, let me tell you about this little one. He's one of the smartest street cats you'll ever meet. He lives in Battersea, and runs a gang called the **BATTERSEA BRUISERS.** Sounds a little scary, I know, but these guys are very much on our side. They keep the alleys and streets of South London safe and have helped Larry on more than one occasion.'

'Give over, Catface.' Socks grinned. 'You're making me blush. Right, lovely to meet you all. I'm off to get a cuppa – no doubt will see you around this weekend.' And with a wink the little cat melted into the crowd, leaving the rest of the party to find their tents.

'Voilà!' Catface beamed as he opened the flap of the tent for the cats to step through.

Inside the cavernous tipi were three sumptuous-looking velvet beds, shaggy rugs on the floor and a wood burner in the centre of the tent, with a chimney that extended to the top peak of the canvas.

THERE WERE ALSO TWO PAIRS OF

SILVER WELLINGTON BOOTS AND PONCHOS
to keep out any rain – gifts from the otter.

'Oh, Lutra, you've outdone yourself!' cried Catface.

'Nonsense, it's a pleasure to have you. Now, make yourselves at home and I'll see you all at the side of the stage to see "*HIS HIGHNESS*" Jonny headline later.' With a wave of her paw, she was off.

'Side of stage passes – they don't give those to just anyone! I told you, sis, Catface and Lutra definitely have the hots for each other,' Silver whispered.

Catface was busy consulting the programme that had been left on his bed. 'It says here that the *CICADA CHOIR OF CALIFORNIA* are playing the *TOADSTOOL*

STAGE – they are excellent, although easier to hear them than see them, I'd wager. Then the **BLACKBIRD QUARTET** are on at six, very tuneful, I'm a big fan. Then we'll get a bite to eat before Jonny is onstage. How does that sound, just the ticket?'

The cats were happy to agree and were about to leave the tent for the day, when they heard someone outside. 'Err, hello? Anyone home?'

'Enteeerrr,' cried Catface in his familiar, pompous boom.

A paw pulled back the flap to reveal one of Jonny's security guards.

'I've got a message here for a **MISS T NINJA CAT,**' he said, delivering the envelope. 'I was told to wait for an answer.'

He skulked out of the tent to loiter outside.

Silver sliced open the top of the envelope with a claw and pulled out the letter. 'It's from Jonny,' he said with surprise. He read out loud:

'Dude, I'm sorry we got off on the wrong paw. It's so cool to be sharing the festival with another legend; I'd love you and the guys to come and watch the set tonight as my guests. And maybe you could come to my trailer to discuss something very

important to do with my
security? I could use your
expertise—'

'This is ridiculous,' interrupted Toto, shutting her eyes in irritation. 'We've come here to have a good time, not to run around after this spoilt brat, and I for one will not desert my friends to go and hang out with—'

'Wait, there's more,' said Silver.

'My personal chef makes a
killer MACARONI CHEESE, I
heard it was your favourite.'

Toto looked down at her paws. 'Well, I suppose I **SHOULD** go and see what he wants, I mean it's in the ninja code, to help strangers in need ...'

'Too right, sis,' Silver laughed. 'You might be a ninja, but you're still a cat ... and a cat's gotta eat!'

CHAPTER 5

Jonny's hired goon was insistent that Toto come alone, so she left Catface and Silver to watch some experimental earwig dancers and arranged to meet them later at the Toadstool Stage.

Toto followed the security guard towards the backstage area. She could feel the festival coming to life around her. She heard a family of ferrets unzipping their tents and noisily making breakfast, she smelled the glorious food being prepared at the stalls (*Silver will probably be first in the queue*, she thought), and she felt the dull thud of vibration as the first bands of the day started to soundcheck on the stages. It was a **SENSORY OVERLOAD** – it excited and thrilled her.

Maybe I've just been taking the whole ninja thing too seriously lately, she thought as the late-morning sun warmed her back. *Catface and Silver are right, I need to lighten up a bit, enjoy myself, and stop being so paranoid. Why not sit down with Jonny? He might be a nitwit, but he's the **BIGGEST ROCK STAR IN THE WORLD!***

Finally, they reached the backstage

VVVVVIP area where Jonny and the band were staying. There was a big crowd at the entrance, made up mostly of local squirrels and pampered London chihuahuas, trying to steal a glimpse into the backstage area to see the rock star. Toto's escort nodded to an exasperated sheepdog, who was working the door but desperately failing to keep order, and Toto was ushered through.

The enclosure had a milk bar to the right (serving Jersey, almond, soya and coconut milk), snack stands dotted around, a huge fire pit in the middle and several pagodas held up by scratch poles draped with catnip and filled with comfy cushions.

At the back were about a dozen or so trailers. Toto's escort knocked on the door of one, which was opened by another security guard, and a couple of nods were exchanged (*Awful lot of nods*, thought Toto) before the ninja was invited in.

Toto could make out the shape of Jonny at the end of the trailer, strumming a guitar and singing a song to himself. The rest of the band were nowhere to be seen, but his security detail lined the sides of the trailer, not entirely without menace. **TOTO'S NINJA INSTINCTS WERE IMMEDIATELY ON FULL ALERT**, but she brushed aside her fears and made her way down to the seating area where Jonny welcomed her like a long-lost friend.

'Here she is! The ninja arrives,' he shouted, like he was trying too hard to make amends. 'Listen, Toto, I wanted to apologise about my behaviour on the train. I know I was a little rude, and even though I know I have, like, loads of cool kick-boxing moves and could probably become a ninja myself, I shouldn't have called you out like that ... So, can we bury the hatchet and, you know, start over?'

Even though he was clearly an idiot who loved himself beyond belief, Toto felt she had to at least make an effort. 'Of course, Jonny, and I really appreciate you saying that.'

'I have to say, man,' he carried on, having barely listened to her reply, 'I think you're one of the only animals who can understand what I'm going through. It's hard being

SO GIFTED AND LOVED, you know, I think *IT'S A CURSE!* No one gets it, and the life of a famous and handsome cat can be so lonely.' As he was explaining this, Jonny's bottom lip quivered, and he started to blub.

Oooh, this is awkward, the ninja thought. She looked around to see if the security guards would help her out, but they stood stone still.

'Err, Jonny, don't worry,' Toto said, as she reached out to pat his shoulder.

Jonny removed the bandana from around his head and blew his nose before continuing, 'So, anyway, I heard what happened on the train and that's why I asked you here. I need you to help look after me this weekend ... Toto, **_I THINK SOMEONE IS TRYING TO GET RID OF ME,_** and they stumbled into your cabin by mistake.'

Toto cleared her throat, and tried to think of the right thing to say. 'Jonny, I know it might be hard for you to believe, but that henchcat was after me ... not you.'

Jonny shook his head. 'Think about it: I'm the most famous cat in the world right now, and there could have been a hundred crazed stalkers on that train. Plus, who's going to think they can get one over on you? No, it's me they were after.' He glanced at his shaded security guards and lowered his voice to add, 'I'm worried my team aren't up to the job. I know you're supposed to be on holiday and all, but I desperately need your help. I'll be forever in your debt. You name it, **_I'LL DO ANYTHING_** to convince you,' he pleaded.

Toto was torn. On the one hand, she was pretty sure no one wanted to harm Jonny. (Although she couldn't blame somebody if they did!) On the other, the **NINJA CODE** meant she had a **DUTY TO PROTECT** those in need. She quickly made up her mind.

'Look, I can't be with you all weekend, but I'll be at the side of the stage for your set and I'll have a chat with your security detail about stepping up procedure.'

'Well, it's not what I asked for, and I normally get what I want ... but OK, deal! Thanks, Toto. Now, I have to soundcheck with the rest of the band, but my chefs made this **MAC AND CHEESE** especially for you, so stick around a while. I'll send my manager in to chat details and I'll catch you later.' He held up a paw, which, despite herself, Toto met with hers in a high five.

'Awesome!' he screamed unnecessarily, then, putting his bandana back on (still covered in snot!), he made a rock 'n' roll fist pump and left.

Toto couldn't resist her favourite dish – she was starving! She helped herself to a massive plate and was chewing happily when she heard the trailer door open behind her.

Ah, Jonny's manag— Toto thought before a rolling pin connected with her head and she fell to the floor.

Toto woke to pitch black all around her, and a very sore head. But the darkness wasn't anything to do with her eyesight – she could feel she was enclosed in a sack. Immediately her **NINJA INSTINCTS** returned and she scolded herself: *Always trust your gut!* How could she have been so stupid to let her guard down and be **TRICKED BY JONNY?** The smell of the macaroni cheese was fresh, so she guessed she was still in the trailer, and she felt movement around her, which had to be Jonny's security guards. If she could just break out of this bag, she'd be able to deal with his mob, and then confront him.

Just as she was about to unsheathe her claws, one of the guards began to speak. She froze. Something in her ninja training told her to be **QUIET AS A MOUSE** and listen ...

'She still out cold?' a gruff voice asked.

Somebody gave Toto a kick, which really hurt but she still kept **ABSOLUTELY SILENT.**

'Yeah, I gave her such a whack earlier, she won't be waking up for a while. So much for the **ALL-POWERFUL NINJA, HA HA.**' Toto recognised the voice of the cat who had come to her tent earlier.

'Good,' came a different voice from the other side of the trailer, 'because it's time for our plan to go into operation and **NOTHING** can get in the way.'

TOTO'S BLOOD RAN COLD. She knew that voice ... and she knew that *smell*. Her brain suddenly clicked. But it couldn't be, could it? The last time she'd heard that annoying voice had been in the middle of the North Sea, in a fight that had only ended when she'd kicked her foe into a barge full of gooey Camembert. That was what she could smell, **CAMEMBERT CHEESE!** The exact same essence as the one she'd picked up on the train, that she couldn't quite put her paw on. And now he was speaking with his real accent, it could only mean one thing: **JONNY'S MANAGER WAS ACTUALLY HER NEMESIS: ARCHDUKE FERDICAT.** He was back!

Her mind was whirring; she needed to get out of here, to warn the others, to get a message to Larry. But as a ninja she knew she had to stay put to learn as much as she could before she acted. She listened carefully as the master criminal addressed his gang.

'My faithful henchcats, you have all done **EXCEPTIONAL** work thus far. We have earned the trust of the biggest rock star on the planet, filmed his new video using our **HYPNOTISING TECHNOLOGY,** and neutralised my nemesis. Tonight is the night when my beautiful plan comes to fruition,' he said, then let out his trademark shrill laugh. **'MMMEEEOOOWWWHAHAHA!'**

Oh, I have NOT missed that cackle, thought Toto.

'When **JONNY IDIOT AND THE SHORT BUMS** take to the stage and play their new song, every single animal in the field **WILL FALL UNDER THE SPELL OF THE HYPNOTISING VIDEO** and obey everything Jonny tells them. They'll then go home and convince their families to watch the video and, hey presto, the whole animal population of the UK, then Europe, then the world will fall under Jonny's spell.'

'Hang on, boss, doesn't that put Jonny and not you in line for world domination?' one member of the gang asked.

MMEEOoWHAHAHA

'You moron. Who controls Jonny? I DO! *MMMEEEOOO WWWHAHAHA!*'

So that's it, thought Toto. *Jonny is just a puppet.* She had to stop that video from being played. But there was no way she could fight ADF *and* his trusted henchcats at the same time. How was she going to escape?

'What do we do with this bag of fur?' a henchcat asked.

'We have to get rid of her. Such a shame – she's an incredible warrior. If only she had seen sense and joined our cause. Still, never mind. Take the bag and throw it in the river.'

'Right you are, boss. Come on, boys, *LET'S SEE IF THIS LITTLE KITTY CAN SWIM.*'

They all let out malevolent laughs as Toto was picked up and hoisted on to someone's shoulder. She heard the door swing open and she was bumped around as they carried her away from the trailer. After a few minutes the noise of the festival became less distinct, and the quiet of the countryside took over.

The gang of cats made their way to the forest at the edge of the festival site, where they could get rid of Toto without anyone seeing.

Now is my chance, the ninja thought to herself. *Get out of this bag, deal with this lot, then get a move on before it's too late.*

She unsheathed her claws to slice open the sack she was being carried in, and with a swish ... nothing happened. She tried again, but the sack stayed firm. *Keep calm,* she told herself but she couldn't stop panic creeping in. Never mind warning the others – if she couldn't get out of this sack, **SHE WAS A GONER.**

CHAPTER 6

'Quit struggling, it won't do you any good,' the cat carrying her laughed, as he swung her round and dumped her on the floor.

Toto could sense she was by a river; she could hear the swirling water down below and smell the moisture in the air. She was furious with herself – how had she been so stupid to relax all her ninja instincts and ignore all the clues? The faint smell of Camembert, the disguised **ARCHDUKE FERDICAT** goading her about bad dreams on the train, the henchcat insisting she visit Jonny alone ... **IT WAS ALL SO OBVIOUS!** And now she was in real danger of drowning before she could warn anyone.

'**CHUCK HER IN QUICK**,' she heard one of the gang say. 'I don't wanna miss that Cicada Choir.'

'Sorry, little ninja, but looks like this is one **PICKLE** you can't get yourself out of ...'

One of the henchcats was just about to kick the sack down the bank of the river when there was a noise from a crop of bushes behind them.

'What are you 'orrible lot up to? Lutra

113

would not take too kindly to you dumping rubbish in her river.'

Toto recognised that cheeky London accent – it was the little kitten who'd snuck in to the festival, **SOCKS!**

She let out a muffled cry for help, and received a quick kick in the side for her troubles.

'Never you mind, **PIPSQUEAK,**' one of the big cats said menacingly. 'If you know what's good for you, turn around now and make your way back to the festival – this don't concern you.'

'That's where we disagree. Poking my nose in where it isn't wanted is the best way to **SNIFF OUT TROUBLE.** I've been following you since you left camp, and I can tell you're up to no good. So, meathead, I'm asking again nicely: **WHAT'S IN THE BAG?**'

Toto could barely believe what she was hearing. She had to admire the little fella; he certainly was brave to stand up to cats who were five times his size. She hoped she could make enough commotion to get his attention and she'd have to keep her paws crossed he'd be able to raise the alarm. She took a deep breath and howled as loud as she could – '**MMMEEEOOOWWW!**' – and waved her paws about. The sack was so thick she worried he wouldn't hear her. She tried again: '**MMEEEOOOWWW!**'

Socks' ears pricked up. Toto could hear him moving slowly towards her.

''Ere, that came from the sack. Is there someone in there?' he demanded.

'No there's not!' one of the gang insisted. 'It's, err, Jonny's fan mail. He gets so much of it that we have to dump it, so we brought it down here to have a fire ...' He trailed off.

Toto could sense that Socks was closer now. Maybe he'd be able to hear her properly? She shouted as loud as she could. **'*SOCKS! IT'S TOTO! GET HELP, ADF IS BACK!*'**

The little cat froze, stared at the sack, then at the henchcats, then at the sack again. The gang stared back. For a second no one was sure what to do, then the leader of the gang screamed, '***GET HIM!***'

Socks bolted and all three of the massive

cats took off after him. In all the **KERFUFFLE,** Toto was knocked by heavy passing paws and the sack tumbled down the river bank, straight into the **FREEZING WATER** below.

The shock of the cold hit Toto hard. Icy water poured in from all sides and Toto desperately paddled her paws to try and stay afloat. She took another futile swipe at the sack but it was no use. The water was rising fast around her neck. Like all cats, **TOTO HATED THE WATER** but at least her ninja training meant that she could hold her breath for a while. She took one last gasp of air, then sank towards the riverbed. Her strength was fading. It seemed there was no hope.

Suddenly, the sack was torn open from above. The last thing Toto was aware of before she blacked out was a strong set of jaws around the scruff of her neck, pulling her towards the surface.

The light was dim, so Toto could only just make out the shadows of her surroundings, but she knew that:

 She was alive (and that deserved a **'WOOHOO'** of titanic proportions)

 Those jaws must have belonged to a **FRIENDLY ANIMAL**, or she definitely wouldn't be alive

 She was wet through, but drying nicely thanks to a **ROARING FIRE** in the corner of the den she found herself waking up in

Trying to get her bearings, she could just make out that she was in a snug room with a low earthen ceiling. The wall nearest to her seemed to be made of small branches and the floor beneath her was carpeted with soft moss. A pot was **BUBBLING** on a stove over the fire. Toto could hear the rushing of the stream that she had just been rescued

from close by. A **SUDDEN SPLASH** caught Toto by surprise – her rescuer had returned from the outside world through an underwater entrance!

'Well, you're a lot more up and at 'em than the last time I saw you ...'

'LUTRA!' Toto said with relief. 'Thank goodness it's you!'

Toto went to get up, intending to rush back to the festival, but moving quickly made her cough up loads of water.

'Woah! Steady there.'

Lutra helped Toto to lie back down, and then added some herbs to a broth simmering on the pot by the fire. She tasted it, then quickly spooned it into a bowl for Toto.

'Now, before you explain to me what on earth is going on, have a bowl of this. You're wet through and unless we warm you up, you'll catch your death of cold and be no use to anyone.'

Toto cautiously raised the spoon to her mouth. The broth's appearance was very odd, with tiny minnow river fish, and tadpoles in it, but it smelled and tasted like nothing she'd ever had before. **IT WAS HOT, SALTY AND HEARTY.** Toto immediately felt rejuvenated.

'Can I ask what's in this?'

'I'm afraid that's an **OTTER FAMILY SECRET.** But it never fails when you've been in chilly water. It's the river herbs that make it so good,' Lutra said, gesturing to the strange plants she'd just added to the pot.

Toto didn't care what they were; they were clearly **DOING THE TRICK.** She felt her strength returning.

'I come here when I need to get away from all the festival hubbub,' Lutra continued. 'Lucky for you, I was just having a **NICE RELAXING SWIM** and a fish when I saw the security guards dumping a sack in the river ... which turned out to be you! What in **HEAVENS** is going on?'

Toto filled Lutra in on the story as quickly as she could. The attack on the train journey, going to Jonny's trailer, ADF's **MASTERPLAN** to control the world of animals through Jonny and his video ...

'If only I'd kept my ninja wits about me. I should have recognised the Archduke from the smell, the voice, the way he moves. I can't believe I've been so, well, blind!'

'Don't beat yourself up,' the otter answered. 'He IS charming. So much so that I signed **ALL THE SECURITY** of the festival over to him. He did such a good pitch, and the quote was very reasonable.'

'But that means—'

'Yes: every security guard working for us in the whole festival is actually working for him. That's a **WHOLE ARMY** we'll have to get through to stop him!'

Toto was aghast. In just a couple of hours Jonny would be onstage and his video would be playing to the whole festival. After that, through him, ADF would have control of hundreds of thousands of animals, and they'd all be doing the work of the most evil genius in the animal kingdom.

The fate of animals everywhere now lay in the hands of a blind ninja and a festival-organising otter ...

CHAPTER 7

Toto had to think fast. 'We've got one thing going for us: ADF and his baddies think I'm dead, so no one will be looking for me or expecting me. Plus, maybe Socks got back in time to raise the alarm to Silver and Catface. Our only chance of stopping this is by preventing Jonny from getting on the main stage. Without him the video will have no impact, as no one will be watching. But how on earth will we get close to him?'

'There are little brooks and streams all over the site that these security guards won't know about. **THIS IS MY FARM,** I've lived here all my life, so I know it like the back of my paw. One stream leads right under the main stage.'

'That's great, but I can't swim,' said Toto mournfully.

'No worries! **YOU CAN RIDE ON MY BACK.** And if we have to go underwater, you can use this to breathe.' Lutra produced a small reed that was almost like a straw.

The thought of being back in the water was a pretty scary one, but Toto nodded her head. 'OK. When we get there, hopefully Catface and Silver will already be at the side of the stage. We'll need all the help we can get. Also, I need to get a message to Larry – if we fail, then he'll need to move fast.'

'I think I can help there too. We should get going, you ready?' the otter asked.

'Well, I'm still pretty chilly, I'm about to get soaked again, I have no idea if we'll be able to stop the **DEADLIEST NINJA OF ALL TIME** in his quest for world domination, and I'm supposed to be on my holidays ... but yes, I'm ready!'

Lutra gave Toto a friendly smile. 'From what Catface has told me about you, you are the **BRAVEST, MOST TALENTED AND COURAGEOUS CAT** he's ever met. And if he thinks highly of you, so do I. You can do this, Toto, and I'll help you all the way.

Now, climb on board.' She crouched down and Toto clambered on to her back. 'Take a deep breath,' Lutra yelled over the roar of the water as they reached the opening of the otter's holt.

Toto gulped and the otter **PLUNGED** them both into the icy water.

This was a far different experience to the

last swim Toto had had to endure. Yes, it was cold, and breathing through the reed felt very strange, but she felt safe and secure riding on Lutra's back. The otter's speed and power in the water was something to behold. Her powerful hind legs kicked **EFFORTLESSLY** through the current, and her tail swished with purpose and power.

After what seemed like an age, the otter surfaced by a bend in the river. 'This is the border of the main festival site. We'll have to take it carefully from here to make sure we're not spotted.'

Toto could sense **THE SMELLS AND THE SOUNDS OF THE FESTIVAL,** and in the distance the Holt Stage stood out against the sky like a temple. The crowd were beginning to congregate to see their idol Jonny strut his stuff.

'First things first: you said you needed to get a message to Larry. I think I have **JUST THE BIRD FOR THE MISSION.'** Lutra let out a kind of bark, which sounded almost like a bird's chirp.

An enormous bird swooped gracefully

across the sky. Lutra turned to Toto and spoke hurriedly, 'This is **FINBAR THE PEREGRINE FALCON.** He's the fastest bird I know, but he's **NOTORIOUSLY ILL-TEMPERED** and he hates city dwellers. He has also been known to ... well, eat small mammals, like you. So, tread carefully.'

'Marvellous,' said Toto, 'I can't wait to meet him.'

The bird perched on a nearby overhanging branch, and said, 'Lutra,' gruffly. Toto wasn't sure if it was a greeting or a question, either way, this bird did not seem to be a happy fellow.

'Finbar, great to see you. Err, how's life? Enjoying the festival?' Lutra winced, knowing what the answer would be.

'Well, you've brought 500,000 animals into my home. It's loud, I can't get any sleep and you told me **I'M NOT ALLOWED TO EAT ANY OF THEM.** I've had better weekends, to be honest.'

'Hmm, it is rather important, if I'm putting on a festival, that you don't consume any of the guests,' the otter answered apologetically.

The huge bird of prey just made a **GRUMBLING** noise.

'Now, Finbar, my old friend, how do you fancy doing your favourite otter a

MASSIVE FAVOUR? We need to get a message to London – **IT'S A MATTER OF LIFE AND DEATH.'**

'LONDON? Forget it,' Finbar chirped back. 'There's a reason I live in the countryside. The last thing I want to do is fly all the way to dirty, polluted, busy London. I haven't flown that far in years, not since my younger days in the Air Force.'

'Finbar, please! I did say it was a matter of life and death!'

Toto suddenly got a sinking feeling that the bird of prey was giving her the once over, as he tapped his **ALARMINGLY LARGE TALONS** on the branch. *Is he thinking about eating me?* she thought anxiously. Luckily Lutra seemed to have picked up on it too.

'This is Toto. **AND NO, YOU CAN'T EAT HER.** She needs your help, which means I need your help. Plus, I know you can get there quicker than any of the other falcons, despite what they say,' she said, knowingly.

That piqued the grumpy bird's interest. **'WHO'S SAYING WHAT?'**

'Oh, it's nothing. It's just the rumour's gone around that you're not as fast as you used to be. Of course, I don't believe a word of it, but it's what the young ones are saying, especially as you lost that race last weeken—'

'That was a false start! I'll show you who's fast!' the falcon cut in. 'Those upstarts are questioning me? Where do you need me to go?'

Lutra nudged Toto forward to explain. When she'd finished, Finbar glowered down at her.

'Good grief, that *is* serious. Don't you worry, little cat. I'll get your boss down here *tout de suite* – that's French for "***VERY FAST***"*!* I go there on me holidays!' He spread his wings and sped into the sky, arcing east towards London.

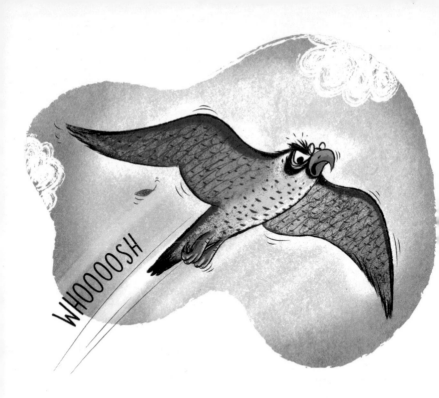

WHOOOOSH

'Red sky, Toto,' Lutra said. 'The sun's setting, which means we're running out of time.'

Jonny would be onstage headlining within the hour – **_THERE WASN'T A MOMENT TO LOSE._**

CHAPTER 8

The otter glided back into the river with the ninja on her back and silently made her way to the Holt Stage. Several times she had to tell Toto to use the reed to breathe, as she submerged to escape the **WATCHFUL EYES** of the black-suited and shaded security guards who patrolled the area.

After half an hour of making their way through the narrow brooks they arrived, just as Lutra had promised, *RIGHT UNDERNEATH THE MAIN STAGE.*

The stage was on one side of the river and extended out over the water, so it almost appeared to float. On the opposite bank, separated by the natural barrier of the river, was the crowd of *HUNDREDS OF THOUSANDS OF ANIMALS.* There was a sudden *ROAR OF EXCITEMENT* and a loud electric guitar strum sounded from the speakers.

'Are we too late?' Toto asked.

'Not yet, the band always come on first and play for a couple of minutes before Jonny makes his *BIG ENTRANCE.* We have to climb up to the side of the stage *AND FAST!*'

Quickly, Lutra swam to the iron bars that made up the frame of the stage and the pair started to scale them. Within a couple of minutes, they were very high and had to be careful of their footing. Even with Toto's training, she didn't fancy a fall from this height.

Finally, they got to the top, by the side of the stage and, clinging on, they peeked over. 'Oh, no,' Lutra sighed as she explained the scene to Toto.

Over the other side of the railings there were all the guests with VIP passes, and between them and the stage there was a row of Archduke Ferdicat's security guards, three cats deep.

'There's no way we'll get through that.

Can you see Silver and Catface?' said Toto.

They were there, in the middle of the VIP crowd. Lutra and Toto carefully climbed down to reach them. Luckily, everyone was so focused on the stage, waiting for Jonny to appear, that nobody noticed them.

By the time the pair got closer to their friends, the **MUSIC WAS DEAFENING** and they could barely hear each other.

'Sis, where have you been? Did you have fun with Jonny?' Silver yelled.

'What? No! Listen, ADF is back, Jonny isn't the bad guy, he's just a pawn!'

'I can't quite hear you,' said Catface. **'JONNY ISN'T A BAD GUY BECAUSE YOU HAD SOME PRAWNS?** Well I, for one, agree

– anyone who serves good quality seafood is all right in my book. Glad you've come to your senses. Ooh! Ooh! *HERE HE COMES!'*

Silver and Catface jumped up and down in excitement, eager to watch Jonny start his set.

Lutra shook her head in exasperation, then quickly tugged on Toto's arm to get her to crouch down. 'A security guard was looking our way!' she explained. Onstage, Jonny had strutted out to pick up his guitar and started to strum.

'HELLO CATSTONBURY! WE ARE JONNY AND THE SHORTHAIRS AND WE ARE HERE TO ROCK YOUR WHISKERS!!!'

The crowd went wild.

'Two, three, four!' The rock star counted the band in and began to sing, to the delight of the throng of animals below.

'Thank goodness,' said Lutra, 'this isn't **"YOU'VE GOT THE CREAM"**, but he's bound to play it soon. How are we going to **STOP** him?'

Toto tried to think of something quickly, but she could smell the familiar scent again. The ninja's sense of smell hadn't let her down: on the opposite side of the stage, in **PRIME POSITION** to take in his masterpiece, but thankfully oblivious to her presence, was a very smug, beaming **ARCHDUKE FERDICAT.**

'Don't suppose I can help, can I?' came a voice from underneath some sound equipment next to them.

'Socks, you made it back! Thank you so much for standing up to those evil cats.'

'No sweat. I ran back to site to try and find you, Lutra, but the security guards all seem to be in league with Jonny's manager so I had to scarper. I've been hiding under here ever si—'

'Oh, no!' Lutra interrupted, as the crowd went wild. 'This is it, the new single, and the video is starting!'

Toto turned to her new friends. 'I need you two to find a way to turn off the screen. I'll take care of Jonny and ADF. Whatever you do, **_DON'T LOOK AT THE VIDEO_** — you'll be mesmerised and fall under Jonny's spell.'

'No problem here,' said Socks with a wink. 'I hate his music, totally overrated.'

'What about you?' asked Lutra.

'I'm almost blind!' laughed Toto. 'What possible effect can it have on me?'

The team went their separate ways, and Toto muscled her way through the crowd to where Catface and Silver were standing. By now Jonny was in full flow, and Toto could sense that something wasn't right. All around her people were in a daze, just staring at the screen. *MAMMA MIA, THEY'RE HYPNOTISED ALREADY!*

Toto needed to act immediately and stop Jonny, but fighting her way through the army of security guards would take too much time and energy, and with so many animals packed into the side of the stage she had no space to somersault over them.

'Hey, sis,' Silver said dozily when she

managed to reach him, 'isn't this new tune something else?'

'Toto, my old chum, give us a cuddle,' she heard Catface drawl, as he swayed on the spot.

'I'm loving Jonny's set,' she replied, as an idea suddenly struck her. **'I LOVE IT SO MUCH THAT I WANT TO CROWD SURF – WILL YOU HELP ME?'**

'Right on, sis, I knew you were rock 'n' roll.'

Catface and Silver supported her hind legs and lifted her up. From there she could hear exactly where on the stage Jonny was, so she lined up her aim, then shouted down to the boys. 'OK, guys, push me up as hard as you can in three, two, one ...'

Toto used the leverage the boys gave her to launch herself, and she **SAILED THROUGH THE AIR,** over the throng of

security guards, towards the rock star.

Onstage, Jonny was preparing for his big chorus. His ego was enormous, but as he looked out at the hundreds of thousands of animals across the bank, even he was surprised by how transfixed the audience were with this new song. He wasn't complaining, but when his manager had insisted it was his new single and promised a really special, expensive music video, Jonny had been surprised – he didn't think it was **THAT** good! Still, who cared? He'd be **EVEN MORE FAMOUS** now, and an American tour beckoned. He sang his favourite line as he drank in the crowd's adoration. 'Life, like cream, can be sour, so sour, but when it's sweet, it's like you ... so goooooooddddddddd

... *AAAARGHOOOOWWW* ...'

The reason the 'good' turned into an 'aaaarghoooowww' was due to the fact that a certain furry Italian ninja had flown through the air and kicked the singer so hard that both **HE AND HIS GUITAR WENT FLYING** to the other side of the stage!

For a second no one quite knew what to do. The band stared at each other in shock (and, if they were honest, they had to try not to laugh) and the security guards gazed in amazement at the scene. The hundreds of thousands in the crowd shook their heads as, at the exact same moment, the mesmerising images from the screen behind the band all went off with a **SHHIIIZZZ.**

Lutra and Socks had knocked out the guard cat in charge of the projector and gnawed through the cable for good measure.

Toto could just about make out the Archduke pulling Jonny to his feet, hidden from the crowd at the other side of the stage.

'Hey, what gives, Toto?' Jonny said. 'I

YEOWWWW

mean, I thought we were friends now? I know the song's not my strongest work, but you're supposed to be looking after me, not knocking me over!'

'Shut up, you wittering fool,' Ferdicat spat at Jonny, then turned to Toto. **'*YOU INTERFERING LITTLE PIPSQUEAK, I WAS TOLD YOU WERE DEAD!*'**

'Sorry to disappoint you, Archduke.' Toto smiled. 'But I think this gig is finished.'

'Quite the contrary. After a brief intermission, I believe an encore is in order. Shame you won't be around to enjoy it. Get her, cats!'

TEN OF ADF'S BEST-TRAINED HENCHCATS descended on Toto. These were not average hired goons, they were professional fighters, and this was going to be tough to get out of.

They circled around the little ninja as she sized up her options. She might not be able to take down all of them, but she was **DETERMINED** to go down swinging ... Before she could work out her moves, she felt the air move around her. *What on earth—*

Flying through the air on ropes attached to the top of the stage, **CATFACE, SILVER, LUTRA AND SOCKS** landed on the guards, knocking them clean out.

'ARRRGGGHHHHHHHHHHHH!'

yelled the Archduke. 'You lot make me sick with your **TEAMWORK** and your **NINJAHOOD** and how much you all support each other, and YOU TWO' – he pointed at Catface and Lutra – 'are so **OBVIOUSLY IN LOVE,** it disgusts me!' An awkward pause followed before ADF continued his rant. 'Anyway, none of this matters. Congratulations, you stopped a video being shown.

SWOOOOOSH

But, duh, I, Archduke Ferdicat, **THE GREATEST NINJA AND CRIMINAL MASTERMIND IN THE WORLD,** am still free and I still control the biggest rock star on the planet, and I have at least two to three evil plans up my sleeve to salvage this. So if you'll excuuuuuuse me, I have a **DRAMATIC EXIT** to sort out!'

ADF grabbed a still-stunned Jonny by his neck and launched up the metal ladder that led to the lighting at the top of the stage.

Across the river, the hundreds of thousands of festivalgoers had started to come out of their stupor as the hypnotising effect of the song and video was wearing off. **THEY WEREN'T HAPPY.** One by one they started to boo, and within a minute it was a cacophony of yelling voices, demanding that Jonny returned to the stage.

Lutra held her head in despair. 'What are we going to do now? My headliner's just been kidnapped – **THIS WILL RUIN THE FESTIVAL!**'

Catface turned to Toto. 'You don't really need me to help catch Ferdi, do you? Let's be honest, I'd be more trouble than I'm worth.'

'No argument here,' replied Toto.

'In that case, I've got an idea. Go get him – good luck, Toto!' And with that, Catface went out onstage to face the booing crowd, leaving the rest of the party to look on stunned.

Toto turned to her brother. **'*READY TO GO AND CATCH SOME BAD GUYS?*'**

'Let's go!' replied Silver, and they bolted for the ladder in pursuit of the Archduke.

'Listen, sis, I'm sorry I didn't believe you,' said Silver as they scampered up as fast as they could. **'YOU WERE RIGHT ALL ALONG** – the train attack, Jonny's security, the smell ...'

'Forget it,' replied Toto. 'Although, how you and Catface didn't recognise Ferdicat is beyond me. At least I've got the excuse of being blind!'

'I guess we were all so in awe of Jonny that we didn't pay his manager any attention. Plus, he **IS A MASTER OF DISGUISE.'**

'That's such a cop-out, but I'll forgive you.' She smiled at her brother.

They reached the very top of the ladder, where a narrow iron walkway ran across the huge Holt Stage. In the middle, attached to the walkway by a thick rope and flapping in the wind, was an enormous hydrogen balloon in the image of Jonny with the band's name written on it.

Toto could hear the thousands of music fans still booing at Jonny's absence from the stage.

The rock star himself sat quivering halfway across the walkway. In front of him, statuesque, but with a murderous look in his eye, was the **MOST DANGEROUS, CLEVER AND DEADLY CAT IN THE WORLD: ARCHDUKE FERDICAT.**

CHAPTER 9

'We've been here before, my little ninja,' the Archduke laughed scornfully. 'Be realistic, you know you can't beat me in combat. **I'VE BESTED YOU BEFORE AND I'LL DO IT AGAIN.** But,' he sighed, almost bored, 'while we're here, and in the best tradition of the baddie asking the heroine how they guessed their evil plan ... humour me: how did you guess my **EVIL PLAN?**'

'It was the cheese that gave you away, the smell of Camembert. I smelled it on the train and knew I recognised it from somewhere.'

The Archduke laughed, but it didn't sound like he found it funny. 'You have no idea how hard it was to get that smell out of my coat. **IT COST A FORTUNE AT THE CAT GROOMER'S**; I can't believe you could still smell the scent. There'll be hell to pay for this.

'I was taunting you on the train, you know. I almost hoped you would guess, just to make the whole thing a bit more fun! Life is so boring when you're an **EVIL GENIUS** and there's hardly anyone as smart as you to spar with. I've only got you and Larry and you're both such **INSUFFERABLE GOODY TWO SHOES!**'

Toto ignored the insult and continued. 'The rest, it has to be said, was sheer luck on my part, and a classic blunder on yours. After one of your gang bashed me over the head, I pretended I was still out cold, and I heard you explain the whole plan to your gang. It's **NINJA 101,** really.'

The Archduke shook his head, disgusted with himself. 'You're right, of course – **NEVER EXPLAIN YOUR WHOLE PLAN WHEN YOUR NEMESIS IS IN THE ROOM ...** I'll never learn. Still, it doesn't matter now. You know, you make life so hard for yourself. I just don't understand why you won't come and work for me?'

'No thank you,' answered Toto, preparing her hero speech. 'I'm perfectly happ—'

'Yes, yes, I wasn't actually asking, I was being rhetorical. We all know you're desperately happy, Larry is a god, humans are great, **BLAH, BLAH, BLAH,** but don't you see, Toto, this plan is perfect! When every animal in the country sees idiot Shorthair here perform his song, I will have control of them, their thoughts and their actions! Then there'll be no crime left for you to fight! What's the downside to that? Anyway, time is ticking, so I'm sorry, I have to chuck you off here pronto and get back to the world domination game!'

'Wait a minute, now I'm really confused!'

All three cats turned to see a snivelling Jonny get to his feet, wiping his nose on his jacket.

'Firstly, Toto, I thought you were supposed to be protecting me? Secondly, YOU' – he gestured to Ferdicat – 'are meant to be my manager, so **WHY HAVE YOU KIDNAPPED ME?** Thirdly, I should be onstage right now in front of my adoring fans, basking in my genius. Lastly, I want some **MILK** and a **COMFORT BLANKET.**'

For a moment, Toto, Silver and ADF looked at each other in amazed silence at Jonny's ego and lack of understanding.

Then the Archduke unleashed a wave of fury at him. '**YOU ARE NOT A GENIUS,** you are just a good-looking idiot. You know nothing, your lyrics are predictable, I had to write most of this album for you, and without me you'd be busking on the streets of Margate ... so **SHUT UP!**'

The rock star burst into tears as the Archduke turned to face Toto. 'Well, shall we dance?'

'Be careful, sis,' Silver cried out.

The gangway was only wide enough for one cat, so there was no room for any error in the duel ahead. One slip at this height would prove fatal, but Toto kept a sure footing as she edged along it to meet her foe. There was hardly any room for **NINJA MOVES** here, so it would be a case of good **OLD-FASHIONED CAT FIGHTING.**

The Archduke sprang towards Toto with a kick to the stomach. It was an expert move and took the wind out of Toto, but using her hind legs she sprang up to leap-frog Ferdicat and kick him hard in the back, sending him sprawling.

'My, my, someone's been practising,' he leered. 'This promises to be a better fight than last time.' Then he shouted,

'*EN-GARDE!*' and launched towards her.

For a few minutes, the two ninjas traded a series of close-quarter blows. Both landed kicks here and punches there, they parried, dodged, blocked and leaped. It was clear to both of them that they were a match for each other, and something very special would be required to win this conquest.

Toto was tiring, but she knew that ADF was too. She needed him to make a mistake she could capitalise on, but he was such an **INCREDIBLE FIGHTER,** she had to think outside of the box. *What's his weak link?* she thought to herself. *Of course: his* **PRIDE** *and his* **EGO!** That was the way to get to him.

'Not so easy when you don't have your

sword with you, is it?' she shouted. 'I thought you were supposed to have thrown me to the ground by now – what's the matter? **NOT AS SHARP AS YOU USED TO BE?**'

'Why, you jumped-up little—' The older cat swung wildly for Toto, leaving himself exposed. She saw the gap: he had a height advantage, but that meant she could get underneath his lunge and connect with his body. She used her last bit of energy on a flurry of blows and finished it off with a swift kick to the ribs, sending Ferdicat sprawling on the gangway. She stood over him, both mighty warriors breathing heavily.

The Archduke slowly dragged himself backwards, grimacing. It was clear that Toto had won the fight, and he was spent.

She held out a paw, offering a momentary
truce to help him to his feet.

'Very good, little one. Maybe one day
we'll make a **_HALF-DECENT BADDIE_** out
of you,' ADF said. 'But sadly, for now, your

morals cloud your judgement; you should **NEVER UNDERESTIMATE A CRIMINAL GENIUS WITH NOTHING TO LOSE.'** With that he leaped up, untethering the huge hydrogen balloon in one paw, and grabbing Jonny by the scruff of his neck with the other, dangling him over the main stage far below.

'You've got yourself a dilemma now, Ninja Cat. **CAPTURE ME, OR SAVE THIS IDIOT?** You can't do both, and he is getting awfully heavy.'

Toto had to admit, it was tempting. The Archduke was finally within her grasp! But she knew she had no choice. She turned to her brother, who shrugged. 'I won't tell if you don't ...' said Silver.

Ferdicat grinned. 'Time's up, Toto. **YOU KNOW EVIL ALWAYS BEATS GOOD — EVIL WILL ALWAYS GO THAT EXTRA MILE TO WIN.** Until we meet again!' He dropped Jonny and the balloon lifted him into the summer night sky.

Instinctively, Toto quickly grabbed a coil of rope lying on the platform, and threw one end to Silver. 'Tie it off!' she shouted and, holding tight to the other end, she **DIVED** over the metal gangway and **PLUMMETED** towards the stage.

Through the roar of the wind, Toto could hear Jonny's screams. Even in this moment of terror, his ego was enormous. '**I'M A GENIUS, AND MY MUSIC IS LIFE-CHANGING ... I DON'T DESERVE TO DIE!'**

MEOOOOOOOW

Toto caught up with him and managed to tie the rope around the cat's waist, even as they fell at high speed. Now, all she could do was pray that her brother could fasten the other end of the rope in time. Sensing the stage floor getting closer and closer, she shut her eyes and positioned herself between Jonny and the ground, a loyal ninja to the last – if she was to get **SQUISHED,** at least she'd save his life.

'IT'S TIED OFFFFF!' she heard her brother call. The rope went taut and they jerked abruptly, suspending them just centimetres from the ground. In a flash, Toto cut through the rope with her claws and they both slumped on to the ground behind two huge speakers. Jonny let out a groan. Toto felt like doing the same. The Archduke had evaded her once again! But at least his plans lay in ruins, and Jonny was alive. The **ANIMAL KINGDOM WAS SAFE** for now, and the festival could carry on with its headline act in one piece.

Then she realised something odd:

the booing has stopped! Not only had it stopped, it had turned into raucous cheering, and there was music playing again. *IF JONNY'S NOT PLAYING, WHO IS?*

Toto lifted her weary limbs and clambered over the speaker to try and make out who was saving the day. As she gazed out over the stage ahead of her, she could make out the silhouette of a figure dancing like he was possessed, and singing without a care in the world. Beyond him, in the fading evening light, the huge crowd seemed to be having the world's best party. She stared in disbelief: even though she could only make out his outline, she was certain ... it was Catface!

Toto jumped down off the speaker and stumbled to the side of the stage where a relieved and grateful Lutra and Socks were waiting. They'd seen the fight from far below, and had feared for Toto's life. They rubbed heads with Toto and piled in for a big hug.

'How did this happen?' the ninja asked them with a laugh, gesturing at Catface strutting his stuff.

'He just strolled on, bold as brass, and asked the crowd if they wanted some good old-fashioned rock 'n' roll!' Socks replied, laughing too.

'*SCRATCH MY SOFA UP! SCRATCH MY SOFA UP!*' the crowd sang back to Catface adoringly.

The song finished and Catface ran to the side of the stage. He lifted Toto right off the floor in celebration. 'I say, if saving the day always involved being a *ROCK STAR,* I'd do it more often. *THIS IS A WORLD OF FUN!*'

From behind him they could hear the

crowd of hundreds of thousands screaming, **'CATFACE! CATFACE!'**

'Please excuse me, I can't leave my public waiting ...' He winked as he turned and walked out onstage again.

'**WE'VE CREATED A MONSTER!**' Lutra said, shaking her head.

Toto laughed along, but as she looked into the night sky, there was just a tiny nagging thought going through her head. There was an evil genius out there, and she wouldn't rest until he was behind bars. **THEY HAD UNFINISHED BUSINESS.**

For his part, the Archduke was thinking pretty much the same thing ... **HE WAS UTTERLY FURIOUS.** For the second time his plans for **WORLD DOMINATION** had gone up in smoke, and no one, NO ONE appreciated how hard it was to put these plans together. He'd been bested in combat, and apparently he *STILL SMELLED OF CAMEMBERT*. (*How was that even possible?*) It was all down to that pesky Ninja Cat. He needed to rethink his strategy; maybe he needed to go after her. He was pondering all this as he sailed through the night sky holding on to his balloon. He wanted to get enough distance between himself and Catstonbury so Toto wouldn't have a clue where he was.

The embarrassment of it all, he thought to himself. *I WAS THE BEST NINJA OF ALL TIME And now? Me, the pick of the litter, beaten by a mere APPRENTICE,*

a runt! I'll never live it down at the Order's reunion. Not that I'm invited to the Order's reunion. They're so discriminatory towards **CRIMINAL MASTERMINDS.** *There's another thing to feel cross about.*

As he was contemplating the different

ways he'd like to get revenge on the little ninja, he looked down and saw another massive music festival. *Hold on a second, this must be the human one going on the same time as Catstonbury! That's my ticket out of here.*

He slowly let the air out of the Jonny and the Shorthairs balloon and spied a row of tour buses. He landed deftly on the roof of one and slid through the skylight. He dropped down on to a very comfy sofa at pretty much the same time as the bus door opened and a human rock band entered the bus, dripping with sweat, having obviously played their gig. The Archduke put on his best '**SAVE ME**' face.

'Hey, guys, look at this, a stray kitty! Must have found his way on to the bus,' one of them shouted to the rest of the band. The tough-looking rock 'n' rollers all crowded around Ferdicat, stroking him, getting him some milk and cuts of meat, and generally **MAKING A FUSS** of him. He **PURRED** away.

'You're not a stray any longer,' one of the band said as he picked the cat up for a cuddle. '**WE'LL TAKE CARE OF YOU.**'

Ferdi smiled to himself. 'Humans are so very predictable. Maybe I'll stay a while, and see what I can do with this band ... **MEEEOOOWWWHAHAHA!**'

CHAPTER 10

The cosy cushioned wheelbarrow rumbled along the country lane, towed as ever by the faithful Gregory, the huge St Bernard. The bright late-morning sun filtered through the willow trees that overhung the road, and everyone felt warm and dozy.

The night had ended in a **STAGGERING SUCCESS.** Catface had stayed on for hours, and was widely regarded as the

GREATEST HEADLINER the festival had seen since the old days of Paws Robinson. Larry had appeared on the back of Finbar the falcon, closely followed by Sheila and the team who had taken ADF's henchcats into custody. And Toto, Silver and Lutra had destroyed the hypnotising video so that it could never be used again.

It had all ended up in a **_HUGE PARTY_** back at Lutra's holt where milk was drunk, old songs were sung and new friendships were cemented. Even Jonny had come along. He'd recovered a bit of his swagger by coming up with a story that made him the hero of the day. He kept telling anyone who would listen that he'd known all along that Ferdicat was posing as his manager, and was just waiting for the right time to take him down – with Toto's help, of course. It was, apparently, all part of his **_GRAND PLAN TO SAVE THE DAY_** and keep his fans safe.

Naturally, most of the media and his fans believed this. The only animals who knew the real story kept quiet at Toto's request when the news cameras had arrived.

'Aren't you a bit miffed?' Silver asked his sister, as the wheelbarrow pulled up at Ottervil station. 'Shouldn't it be us – I mean, *you* – getting all this attention?'

'Brother, the last thing I want is attention. Jonny's welcome to it. I just want to get home and **SLEEP FOR A WEEK,** then go back to normal ninja duties. They're a lot safer than this **ROCK 'N' ROLL** game!'

Jonny and the Shorthairs were already on the platform, just about to board the train. Nana, the bass player, came over to Catface. 'You were **INCREDIBLE** last night, Catface. We've never seen a crowd like it.'

'Oh, stuff and nonsense ... Was I, really? I mean, I suppose I was a rat choirboy back in the day, I represented Ratborough several times at the **RODENT CHOIR OF THE YEAR COMPETITION.'** He beamed proudly.

Nana leaned into him. 'Listen, keep it

quiet, but some of the band are thinking about leaving Jonny. He's a bit of a bore to work with, because he loves himself so much. If you ever fancy giving this a go seriously, well, get in touch.'

'Oh, that's marvellous,' replied a very chuffed Catface. 'I say, do you think there's a market for old rat standards, reworked? You know, like *"IT'S A LONG WAY TO RATTERRARY"*, *"RATTY DAYS ARE HERE AGAIN"*, *"I DO LIKE TO BE BESIDE THE GUTTER"* ?' he asked hopefully.

'Err, probably not,' said Nana apologetically before she hopped on board the train. 'Best keep those ones to yourself, but get in touch if you ever want to do some new stuff. *YOU ARE ONE COOL CAT/RAT.*'

The man of the hour turned to Lutra to say goodbye. 'Well, my old, err, friend, great to see you again.'

'Thank you, Catface. Without you the festival would have been a **DISASTER.** And YOU three' – she turned to Toto, Silver and Socks – 'if it wasn't for you three, there'd be no festival and we'd all be under Ferdicat's spell. You've got a **FRIEND** in the West Country for life.' She cuddled the three little cats, and then shared a shy smile with Catface. It really *did* seem as though she liked him.

'All aboard!' the conductor of the train shouted. 'Next station is the human town of Reading!'

The three little cats hurried on to the

train as Catface was looking mournful. 'Goodbye, Lutra, see you soon, maybe in the autumn for a spot of fishing?' he asked hopefully.

'I'd like that very much,' she replied as she **KISSED** him on the cheek.

From the window of the train, the three cats all fell about **WHOOPING AND CHEERING.** A minute later, Catface sat down next to them in stunned silence, all three looking eagerly at him.

'Told you they liked each other.' Silver nudged his sister. 'I've got an intuition about these things.'

'Yeah, you picked up on that, but couldn't recognise the criminal you saw just a matter of months ago. Your talent is uncanny!'

Toto laughed, and gave her brother a nibble on the ear.

One by one the cats settled down for the journey home and after a while, each fell in to a **_PEACEFUL AFTERNOON DOZE._**

They woke only as the train pulled into London's Paddington station, and the friends disembarked to go their separate ways.

Catface had made an appointment with a fox who owned a music management company – 'Just to explore my options'. Toto and Silver were looking forward to getting back to their human mamma and papa for some **QUALITY SOFA TIME.**

Toto turned to Socks to say goodbye. 'I suppose you'll be getting home now, too? I bet your family are missing you.'

From behind Socks, Catface made a gesture with his paw across his throat as if to tell her to be quiet, but it wasn't bright enough in the station for her to make out his signal.

'Err, not exactly,' Socks replied. 'I live in Battersea – as in the cat's home. Dogs live there too, but they're noisy blighters so we keep to the quiet part of the building.'

'But where are your **HUMAN** family?' asked Silver.

'Well, I suppose I don't have one. Just me mates at the home and the Battersea Bruisers.'

'Remind you of anyone?' Catface smiled knowingly at the cats, as they, too, had been without a family until they'd been adopted from Italy.

'Anyway,' Socks chirped up, 'an honour to work with you both, hope to see you around soon.' He gave the cats a firm handshake, picked up his knapsack and headed off to the Animal Tube.

The cats turned to each other. 'Are you thinking what I'm thinking?' Toto asked her brother.

'Yep! What's for dinner?' Silver replied. 'Joke!' Then he ran after their new kitten friend. **'HEY, SOCKS! HOW DO YOU FANCY A MOVE NORTH OF THE RIVER?'**

EPILOGUE

Mamma and Papa had just returned from a weekend at the Glastonbury music festival and were exhausted! They could think of nothing more now than *A WARM BATH, A CUDDLE* with their TWO favourite cats and *AN EARLY NIGHT.*

As Papa took the suitcases full of very dirty clothes upstairs, Mamma went to put the kettle on and find her furry friends. **BUT SHE COULDN'T SPOT THEM ANYWHERE!** She tried the **KITCHEN** (where they'd normally be), their little **HIDEY-HOLES** under the beds, the **SOFAS** in the living room. No sign of them. It was then she heard a faint but distinct meow coming from the **ATTIC ROOM.**

She climbed the stairs to the attic and found her cats curled up with a cute **TABBY AND WHITE KITTEN** nestled between them, meowing quietly. If she didn't know better, she could have sworn it was smiling at her!

'Papa, I think our family might have grown,' she called down the stairs, and picked the kitten up in her arms to give it a welcome cuddle. 'Who are you?' she asked.

PUUUURRRRRRR

The new kitten gave her a little lick. Mamma put him on her shoulder and started to walk downstairs.

Looking back at his adopted brother and sister, Socks gave them a beaming grin. Toto returned a thumbs up. 'Welcome to the family!'

THE END

HAVE YOU READ TOTO'S OTHER ADVENTURES?

ALSO AVAILABLE IN AUDIO –
READ BY **DERMOT** HIMSELF!

AUTHOR Q AND A
MEET DERMOT!

Where did you grow up?

I was born in Colchester – my parents moved there because they wanted to bring their kids up just outside London. My parents came over from Ireland in the late 1960s.

What was home like?

Really lovely. There were a lot of people the same age as my parents that had kids, and we all went to the local village primary school. But we lived a double life! Every weekend we'd come up to London and that was all about the church, the pub and the GAA – the Gaelic Athletic Association. We'd be round my auntie's house for rashers of bacon in the morning and then roast beef in the afternoon. Being Catholic and brought up Catholic in a little town like Colchester, we all stayed together.

Did you enjoy reading as a child?

Yes, and both my parents are big readers. My dad is great – he's a born storyteller. He read us old Irish fairy stories that he was passing on. He even wrote a little book about two owls for my niece when she was younger.

Fantastic Mr Fox was always my favourite book when I was growing up. I also really loved Raymond Briggs – *The Snowman and Father Christmas* especially.

Did you visit the library as a child?

All the time. Every Saturday when I was at primary school, all my friends would be off playing football. But I had to go to catechism classes instead, so to make up for it, my Dad would take me to BHS café for strawberry flan and then he'd take me to the library in Colchester – it was a brilliant library. I loved looking at the local papers on the old microfiche, and as I got older, it was just a great place to go and study.

ACKNOWLEDGEMENTS

Well, as always, the big thanks have to go to the big cats.

Toto, you are a dear friend and an inspiration for how to live a life. Fearless and brave, you never let your condition hold you back. You are trusting and loving to all you meet.

Most humans could learn a thing or two from you ... and you're only awake for four hours a day.

Silverboy, we still miss you every day and we know you're looking down smiling and running riot with that beautiful bushy tail of yours.

Socks, thanks for finally calming down, it's great to have you as part of the family and we hugely appreciate the squeaky purrs every time we come home.

To Dee, for being my counsel and sounding board on all things Toto and the world, and for generally 'Winston-ing' the hell out of life.

To my Mam, Maria, and Dad, Sean, for filling our house with words and wonder and raising us on the songs and stories which make up our history.

John, Jonny, Jess and Arqam at JNM for pushing the ocean back with a broom and helping me find time to indulge this passion. And to Liz Matthews and all at LMPR for helping me be able to shout about it.

To the wonderful human-being that is Nick East, illustrator and friend, for your talent in bringing Toto and all the gang to life. And for being the kind, curious soul that you are. The world is lucky to have you.

To all my friends at Hachette, because that in truth is how I feel every time I visit. In particular, thanks to Anne McNeil for the unwavering, stateswoman-like support, Alison Padley for the hutzpah and the vision, and to my Editor, the far-far-too-intelligent-for-my-liking sensei that is Kate Agar. Who is always right, editorially and actually. On point!

Plus, to Fritha Lindquist, who must be some kind of superhero, as she's always in ten places at the same time ... extraordinary.

To the good souls at Battersea Dogs and Cats home, ditto the Dogs Trust, Celia Hammond, RSPCA, HSI, Spana, and any animal welfare charity.

To Fran, the cat whisperer, Chantel and all at Village Vets

To all the people who run and work at book festivals, schools and bookshops. Since I started writing about Toto and travelling around the country, I've been blown away by your passion, energy and devotion to getting kids reading. Thank you for welcoming me ... and for the excellent standard of cake.

And, lastly, to any of those kids reading this, thanks for all the feedback and support you've given Toto. Never stop reading, writing, creating. It doesn't matter how many mistakes you make. Just use that imagination and see where it takes you.

DERMOT O'LEARY'S

television and radio work has made
him a household name.

Dermot started his career on T4 for Channel 4, and has presented shows for both ITV and the BBC. His best-known work includes ten series of The X Factor, Big Brother's Little Brother, BBC3's First Time Voters Question Time, Unicef's Soccer Aid, the RTS Award winning 'Live from Space' season following the International Space Station's orbit of the Earth in 2014 and the Brit Awards which he presented with Emma Willis in 2016.

2017 saw Dermot launch his new Saturday morning show on BBC Radio 2, 'Saturday Breakfast with Dermot O'Leary'. Previously in the Saturday afternoon slot, 'The Dermot O'Leary Show' won three Sony Radio Awards and was well known for its support of new and emerging bands.

2018 saw Dermot host the National Television Awards for the ninth time. He also joined Kirsty Young and Huw Edwards to host the BBC's coverage of the Royal Wedding in front of an audience of 13 million people.

In 2019, he presented the Explorers episodes of the BBC's 'Icons: The Greatest Person of the 20th Century', and ITV's 'Small Fortune'.

Toto the Ninja Cat and the Superstar Catastrophe is Dermot's third children's book. He lives in London with his wife Dee and their cats Socks and, of course, Toto.